ABOUT THE AUTHOR

A self-made man, Michael Rosenblum is a popular motivational speaker and workshop leader. Additionally, he is a sought-after guest expert on TV and radio in the US and Canada. Born in Dallas, Texas, he was raised in the Washington, D.C. area. After graduating from the University of Missouri, Rosenblum moved to Chicago, where he began a career in media sales, eventually creating and selling three travel magazines. He next set his sights on the competitive Chicago real estate market, quickly establishing himself as one of America's most successful brokers. He is grateful to be able to share what he's learned about fear and faith with young readers.

ABOUT THE ILLUSTRATOR

As a child, Polina Poluektova loved art and enjoyed creating imaginary worlds. Her main sources of inspiration were classic fairy tales, folklore, nature and animals, both real and mythical. She is a graduate of the prestigious Academy of Art in San Francisco and lives in Switzerland, where she is a professional illustrator.

D1366479

Created & Written by Michael Rosenblum
Illustrated by Polina Poluektova

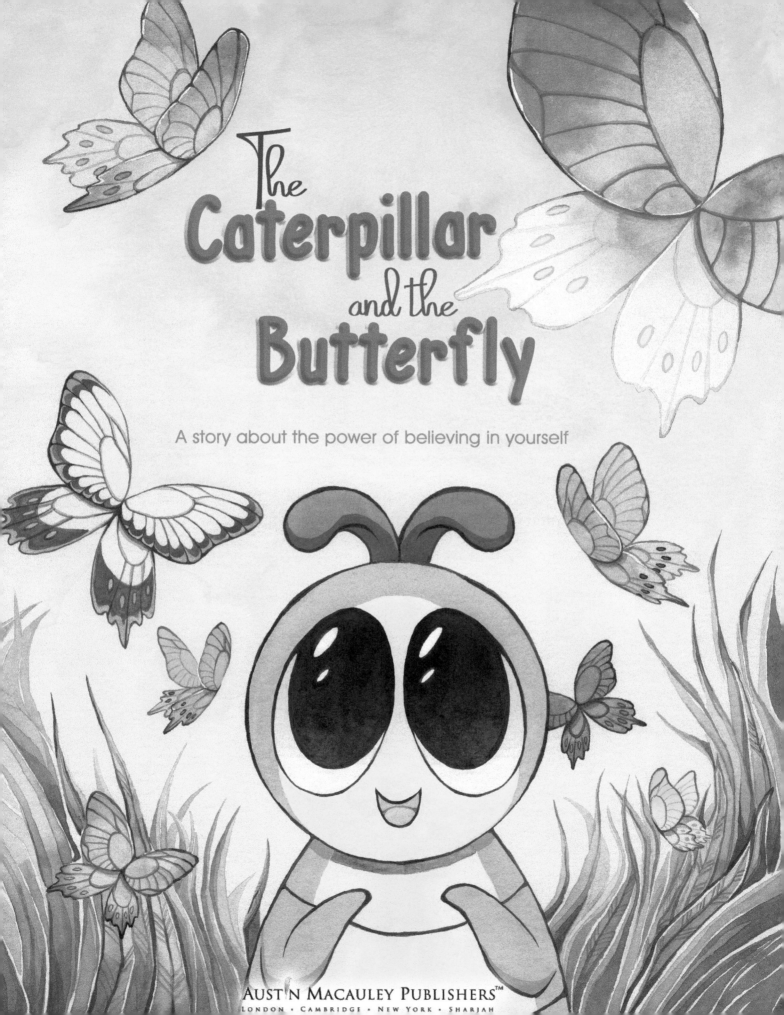

The Caterpillar and the Butterfly

A story about the power of believing in yourself

AUSTIN MACAULEY PUBLISHERS™

LONDON · CAMBRIDGE · NEW YORK · SHARJAH

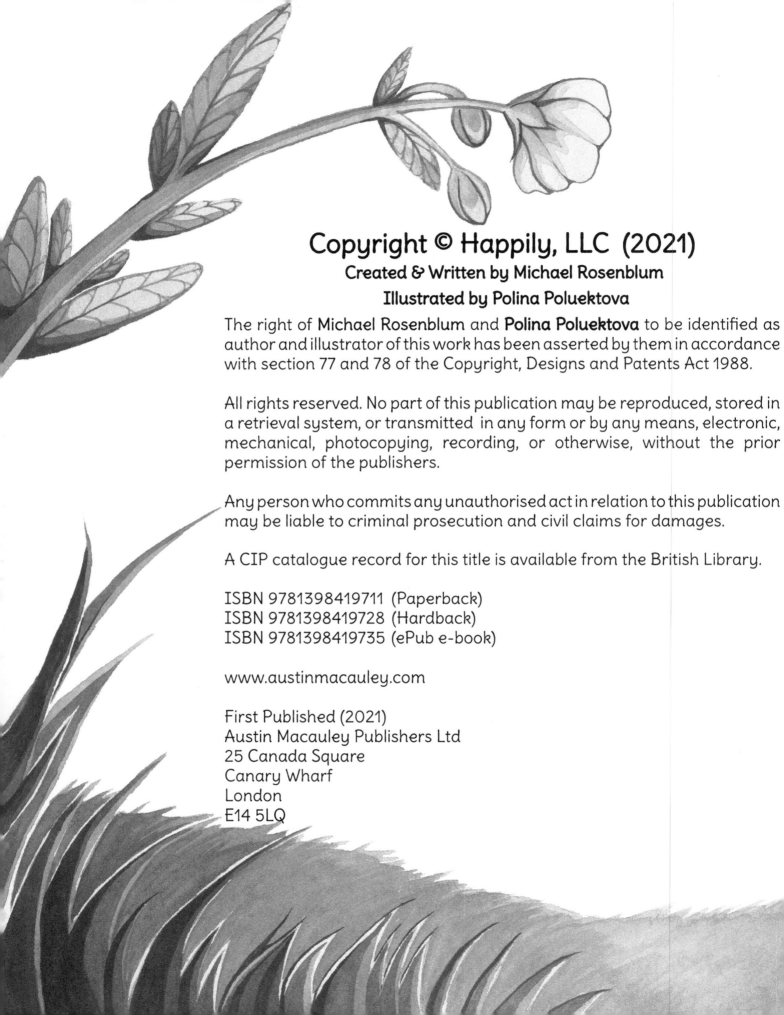

A CIP catalogue record for this title is available from the British Library.

ISBN 9781398419711 (Paperback)
ISBN 9781398419728 (Hardback)
ISBN 9781398419735 (ePub e-book)

www.austinmacauley.com

First Published (2021)
Austin Macauley Publishers Ltd
25 Canada Square
Canary Wharf
London
E14 5LQ

In dedication to Bernice.

Our friendship was magical.

Your teachings were brilliant.

I adored our time together.

You will always be a butterfly to me...

I love you.

In a garden lived a little caterpillar.

Afraid of so many things,
the other critters named it Fear.

One day, Fear saw the most magical
butterfly and watched it from behind
the grass.

The butterfly landed nearby on a flower.

"Hello! Would you like to play?"

Fear coiled into a ball.

"Don't be afraid. My name is Faith.
I am a friend."

Fear did not answer.

"What's your name, little caterpillar?
Please tell me what's wrong."

"My name is Fear and I feel sad."

"Why?" asked Faith.

"Because I'm afraid of many things,"
Fear explained.

"What are you afraid of?"

"Other critters, lightning storms, being bullied,
making friends, trying new things."

"I understand how you feel. I won't let anything happen to you. Come play with me."

With the help of Faith, Fear tried new things and made new friends.

Each day, Fear became a little braver.

One day, Fear said to Faith,

"You make it seem so easy.

I wish I felt as free from worry as you do.

I wish I could fly high like you."

Faith smiled and said,
"I was once just like you.
One day you will be just like me."

"But how will that happen?"
Fear asked.

Faith flew down and sat
beside Fear.

"You need to try new things,
even when you are afraid."

"You need to be kind,
even when you are afraid."

"Most of all, you need to believe in yourself, even when you are afraid."

"When you can do these things, you will have the power to fly!"

That night,
Fear thought about what Faith said.

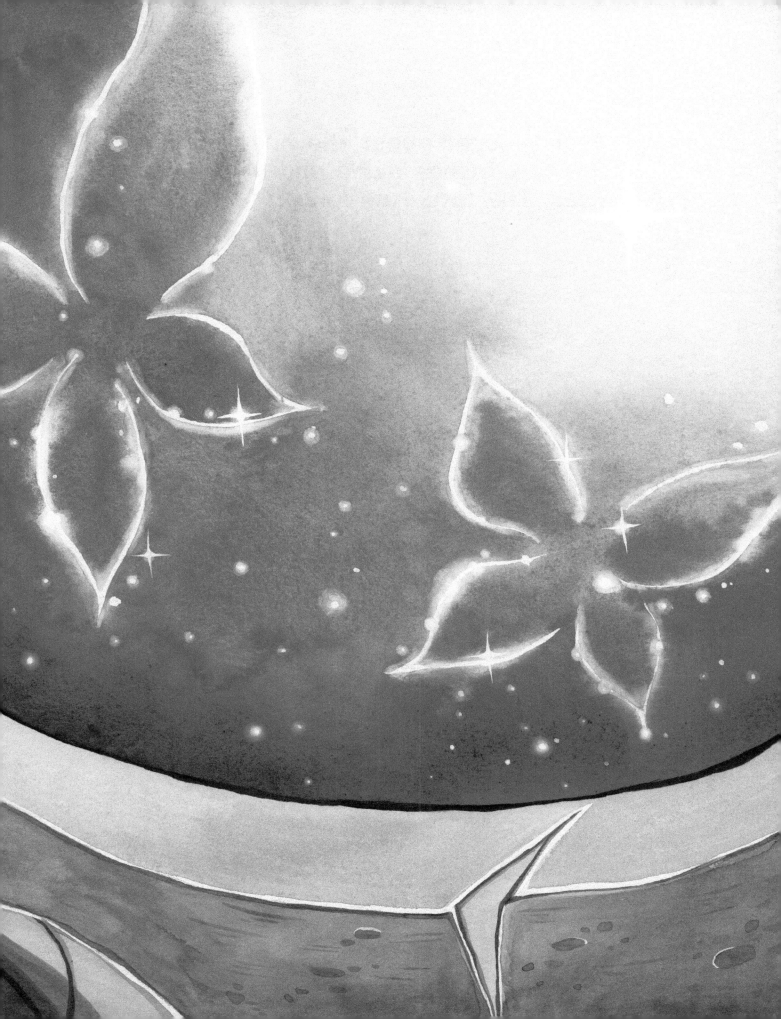

Fear thought about the past months, the new friends made and all the new experiences. The future no longer seemed as scary.

Fear decided to start believing in Faith. Suddenly sleepy, Fear took a long, cozy nap and dreamed of what could be.

In the new day,
Fear found the magic of Faith...

...and started to fly.

Happily ever... Always!

CPSIA information can be obtained
at www.ICGtesting.com
Printed in the USA
BVHW021911260821
615347BV00018B/597